ALEX'S
Adventures
at the Harbor

Eduard Delgado ★ *Francesc Rovira*

Derrydale Books

New York

2

"Wouldn't you like to go around the world in a ship as big as that?"

Looking out over the calm waters of the harbor filled with big liners, freighters, and fishing boats all coming and going, Alex started to dream of great voyages to far-off lands.

3

But even in quiet harbors things can happen from time to time. Today, because of a mistake, a freighter went right in front of a big passenger ship and there was no way to stop them from banging into each other.

4

"Look, they've had a collision!
Let's row over to see if we can
help the passengers."

5

What a surprise! The cargo ship was carrying animals for the zoo. I wonder if lions can swim.

6

"Look, a crocodile this big! Quick, row as fast as you can!"

7

"Go back, go back! The crocodile is after us!"

8

While the fishermen were filling up their boat with fish they had caught in their nets, the rescue job got underway. The porpoises took the opportunity to leap and play. The other animals were not too scared, they were just a bit puzzled.

"Phew!
We've just
escaped by the
skin of our teeth!
What a lot of big
teeth he has!"

10

What a fright! Alex and his friends got out of the boat and scrambled to safety at the very moment a sailor managed to catch the crocodile.

Little by little things quieted down again. The crew of the freighter had been saved, most of the animals had been hoisted up on board, and the porpoises went on with their games. Since Alex wasn't scared anymore he decided to take a swim.

The fishing boat was so full of fish it could hardly move through the water. It's a good thing there aren't any big waves in the harbor! While the sailors were collecting the rest of their belongings, Alex went swimming underwater with the porpoises and discovered that there was lots of junk on the bottom of the harbor.

"Faster, Alex! You'll win the race!"

16

"Captain, we're sinking!" The little
fishing boat began to sink under its
heavy load of fish, but Alex was so busy
with his games that he didn't see what
was happening.

The television reporters interviewed Alex
and his friends about what had happened.
What a surprise their parents are going to
get when they appear on the news!

"The crocodile was chasing us and…"

ALEX'S FIVE GAMES IN THE HARBOR

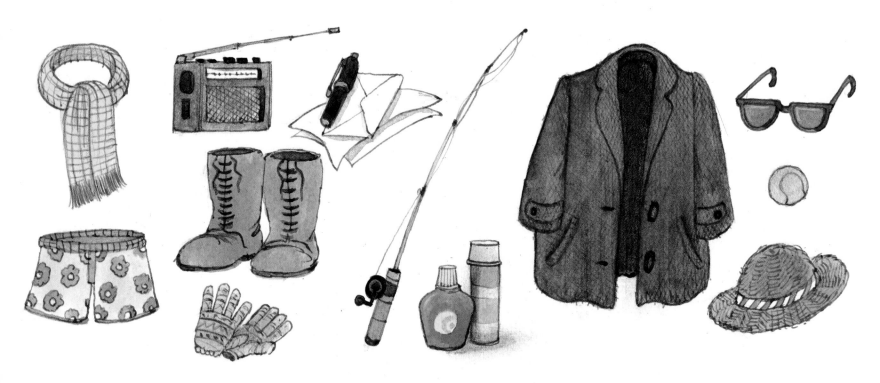

1. ALEX'S TRAVEL GAME

Alex would like to spend his vacation fishing and sunbathing on a tropical island. Of all the things in the drawings, point to those you think would be handy on a voyage like that. Which ones wouldn't be too useful?

2. ALEX'S ANIMAL GAME

Without counting the fish in the fishing nets, the drawings in this book include 103 animals:

64 birds	5 cats
16 fish	3 lions
12 porpoises	3 crocodiles

Who is going to be first to discover them all?